SCOOBY-DOO!™

AND THE CARNIVAL CREEP

Written by Sonia Sander
Illustrated by Duendes del Sur

SCHOLASTIC INC.
New York   Toronto   London   Auckland
Sydney   Mexico City   New Delhi   Hong Kong

ISBN 978-0-545-30445-0

Designed by Michael Massen

12 11 10 9 8 7 6 5 4 3 2 1   11 12 13 14 15/0

Printed in U.S.A.   40
First printing, January 2011

"Like, if we don't hurry up," said Shaggy, "we'll miss out on all the good food."

Daphne laughed. "Guys, we're at a carnival. They never run out of food."

"Come on, gang!" called Fred. "I see the owner at the ticket booth."

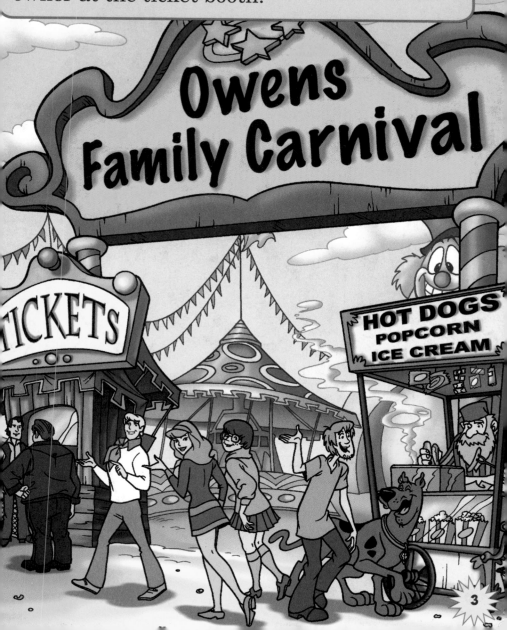

TICKETS

Owens Family Carnival

HOT DOGS
POPCORN
ICE CREAM

Orville Owens and his sons, Otis and Oscar, were waiting for the gang at the ticket booth. "Welcome to our carnival!" Orville called out. "That is, Oscar's carnival. He's taking over for me."

"How about we start our tour with the haunted house?" asked Oscar.

"Raunted rouse? Ro ray!" cried Scooby.

"Like, count us out," said Shaggy. "Scooby and I are heading to the fun house."

ICE CREAM

5

Oscar took Fred, Daphne, and Velma into the library of the haunted house.

"There's a secret door, but I bet you'll never guess how to open it," said Oscar.

He reached into the fake fire and took out a log. With that, the fireplace spun around.

All of a sudden, they were in a dressing room

"Oh, dear," said Oscar. "It's usually not this messy."

"Maybe someone was in a hurry," said Daphne.

"Even so, it should never be this bad," said Oscar. Plus, it looks like a few things are missing."

Shaggy and Scooby were having a ball in the fun house.

"Check me out in this mirror!" called Shaggy. "How cool is it that we're the only ones in the fun house?"

"Ruh-huh!" barked Scooby.

But they weren't the only ones in the fun house. . . .

The Carnival Creep was there, too!
"Zoinks! Run, Scooby!" cried Shaggy.
"Like, this place just went from funsville to creepsville!"
Scooby and Shaggy raced out of the fun house.

The two buddies found the rest of the gang. They told them about the Carnival Creep.

"Like, I've had enough of this creepy carnival," said Shaggy.

"Sorry, but we've got a mystery to solve," said Fred.

"Ro ray!" barked Scooby.

"Not even for a Scooby Snack?" asked Daphne.

Scooby could never say no to a Scooby Snack.
The gang split up to look for clues.
"Scoob and I are going to check out the games,"
said Shaggy. "Like, how creepy could that be?"

But — *ruh-roh* — the Carnival Creep
popped up there, too!

"Jinkies, it looks like there's a string tied to this milk can," said Velma.

"When the milk can fell down, it pulled up the fake Creep," Daphne said.

"Great job finding that clue!" said Fred. "Now we know the Creep is a fake."

All of a sudden, the gang heard screams from the Ferris wheel.

The Carnival Creep was jumping from one car to another!

"Jeepers, it looks like there's a real Creep after all!" said Daphne.

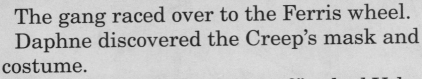

The gang raced over to the Ferris wheel. Daphne discovered the Creep's mask and costume.

"Otis, did you see the Creep?" asked Velma.

"I'm afraid not," said Otis, wiping his neck. "I've been too busy running the wheel."

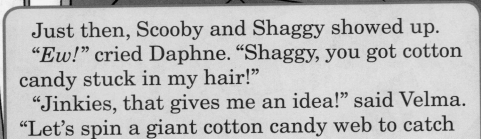

Just then, Scooby and Shaggy showed up.
"*Ew!*" cried Daphne. "Shaggy, you got cotton candy stuck in my hair!"

"Jinkies, that gives me an idea!" said Velma. "Let's spin a giant cotton candy web to catch that Creep!"

BUMPER CAR

Scooby and Shaggy did not want to be bait for another one of the gang's traps. But when Daphne mentioned more cotton candy, they couldn't say no.

"Slide faster, Scoob!" cried Shaggy. "Don't let that creepy Creep catch you!"

The rest of the gang was ready.
They spun a web big enough to catch a Creep!
Before he knew what hit him, the Creep was stuck in a giant web of pink cotton candy.
"Gotcha!" Fred declared.

"I know who you are, Creep," said Velma. "The green makeup on your neck gave you away."

Velma pulled off the mask to reveal . . . Otis!

"I would've gotten away with it if it weren't for you meddling kids," said Otis. "The carnival would have closed, and then *I* could have been the new owner."

With the mystery solved, it was time to kick back and enjoy the carnival! "Scooby-Dooby-Doo!" shouted Scooby.